To my girls, LaLayna and Lola. — CJ

Little ★ BOOST is published by
Picture Window Books, A Capstone Imprint
151 Good Counsel Drive, P.O. Box 669
Mankato, Minnesota 56002
www.capstonepub.com

Library of Congress Cataloging-in-Publication Data
Jones, Christianne C.
Maybe when I'm bigger/by Christianne Jones;
illustrated by Mark Chambers.
p. cm. — (Little boost)
ISBN 978-1-4048-6168-8 (library binding)
[1. Growth—Fiction.] I. Chambers, Mark, ill. II. Title.
PZ7.J6823May 2011
[E]—dc22   2010004788

Summary: When Janey gets tired of hearing
that she is not big enough to do the fun
things she wants to do, she decides that
she is not big enough to do boring things too.

Creative Director: Heather Kindseth
Art Direction/Graphic Design: Kay Fraser

MAYBE
When
I'm
BIGGER

by Christianne Jones   illustrated by Mark Chambers

PICTURE WINDOW BOOKS
a capstone imprint

Janey was big enough to do most things herself.

She could get dressed.

She could use the potty chair.

She could even fix her own breakfast.

However, Janey was still a little too
small for some things.

"I'm taking a taxi to the mall," Janey said.

"I don't think so," her dad replied.
"Maybe when you're bigger."

"I'm going on the new
roller coaster," Janey said.

"You're too small," her brother replied.
"Maybe when you're bigger."

"I'm not **BIG** enough for anything **fun**," Janey complained one day.

"That's it!" she declared. "If I'm not big enough for the fun stuff, I'm not big enough for the boring stuff, either."

And so it began.

Her mom said, "Janey, clean your room."

Janey replied, "Not today.
Maybe when I'm BIGGER."

Her dad said,
"Janey, eat your
vegetables!"

Janey replied, "I don't think so.
Maybe when I'm BIGGER."

Her mom said,
"Janey, it's time
for a bath."

Janey replied, "I'm too **small.**

Maybe when I'm BIGGER."

"Janey, you are not acting like a big girl," her mom said.

"Maybe I'm not a BIG GIRL!" Janey replied.

"Really?" her dad asked.

"**Really**," Janey said.

The next day was Janey's first day
of preschool. She was VERY excited!

"Where are you going?"
her mom asked.

"To school!" Janey yelled.

"Only big girls go to school," her dad said.

"But I am a BIG GIRL!"

Janey exclaimed.

"That's not what you said yesterday,"
her dad reminded her.

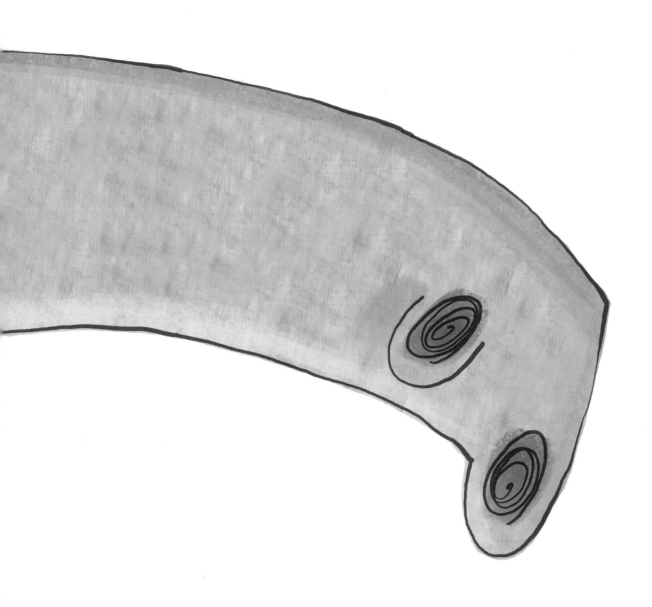

"And you sure haven't been acting like a big girl," her mom said.

"**Well,** I changed **my mind,**"

Janey said.

"Really?" her dad asked.

"Really," Janey said. "I may not be **BIG enough** for some things ...

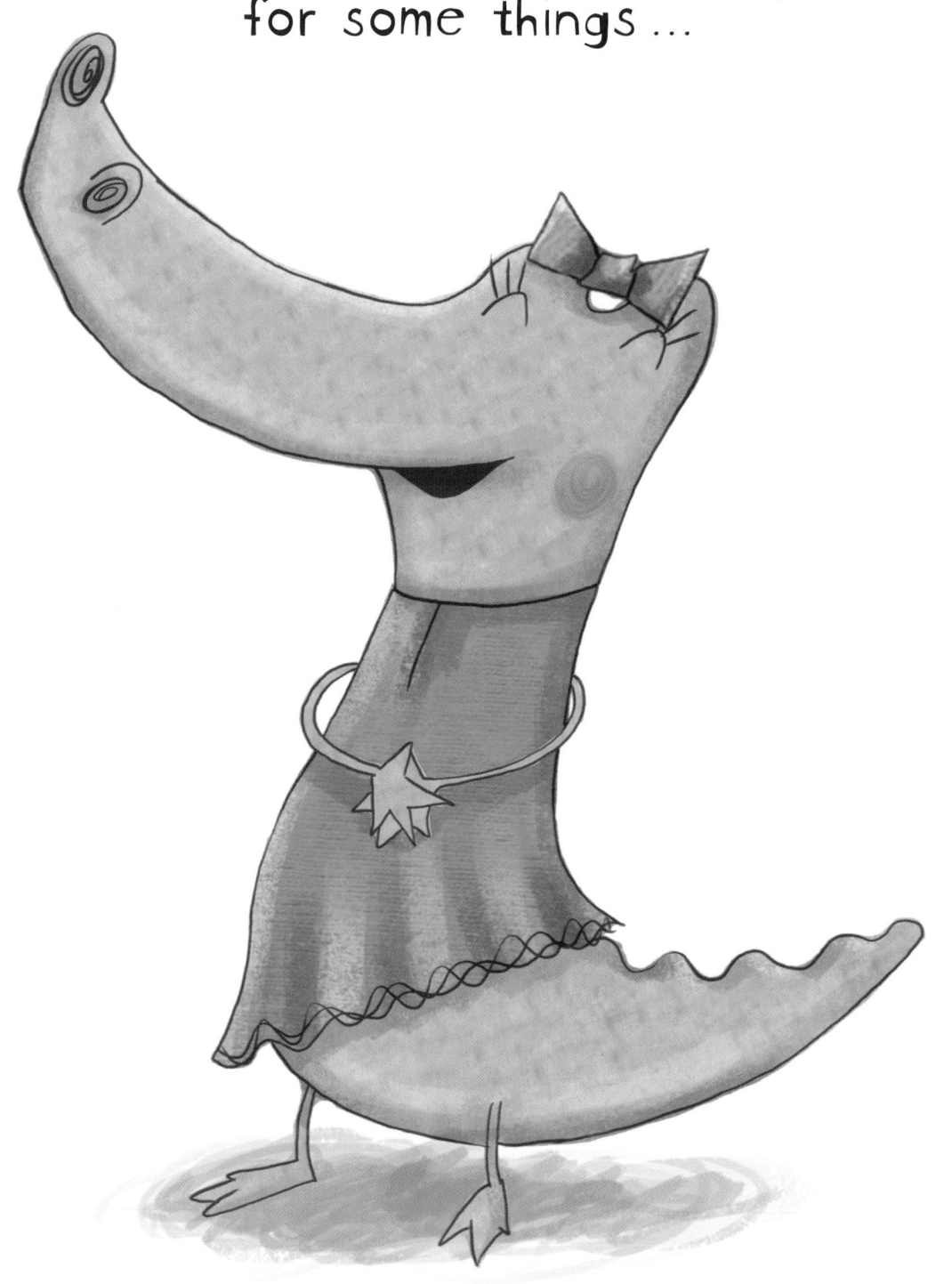

". . . but I'm just BIG enough for now."